Celebrations in My World

Victoria Day

Lynn Peppas

Crabtree Publishing Company

www.crabtreebooks.com

Crabtree Publishing Company

www.crabtreebooks.com

Author: Lynn Peppas

Editorial director: Kathy Middleton

Editor: Molly Aloian

Proofreader: Crystal Sikkens

Photo research: Allison Napier,
Samara Parent

Design: Samara Parent

Print coordinator: Katherine Berti

Production coordinator: Samara Parent

Prepress technician: Samara Parent

Photographs:
© Gunnar Freyr Steinsson / Alamy: page 25
© Wangkun Jia | Dreamstime.com: page 13
© Minister of Canadian Heritage, 2011: page 10
Object Gear: page 14 (sheet music)
Shutterstock.com: cover (except bottom right), pages 6,
  14, 18, 19, 21, 30 (bottom), 31 (bottom); Liudmila
  Cherniak: page 4; skphotography: page 11; rook76:
  page 15; Elena Elisseeva: page 22
Thinkstock.com: pages 5, 8, 9, 12, 17, 20, 23, 24, 26,
  28, 29, 30 (top), 31 (top)
Wikimedia Commons: Alexander Bassano: cover
  (bottom right); ©Dave Beuh: title page;
  © Mohammad Jangda: page 16; Library and
Archives Canada: pages 7, 27

Library and Archives Canada Cataloguing in Publication

Peppas, Lynn
   Victoria Day / Lynn Peppas.

(Celebrations in my world)
Includes index.
Issued also in electronic format.
ISBN 978-0-7787-4088-9 (bound).--ISBN 978-0-7787-4093-3 (pbk.)

   1. Victoria Day--Juvenile literature. I. Title. II. Series:
Celebrations in my world

6502

GT4813.A2P47 2012   j394.262   C2012-900896-6

Library of Congress Cataloging-in-Publication Data

Peppas, Lynn.
   Victoria Day / Lynn Peppas.
     p. cm. -- (Celebrations in my world)
  Includes index.
  ISBN 978-0-7787-4088-9 (reinforced library binding : alk. paper) --
ISBN 978-0-7787-4093-3 (pbk. : alk. paper) -- ISBN 978-1-4271-7847-3
(electronic pdf) -- ISBN 978-1-4271-7962-3 (electronic html)
  1. Victoria Day--Juvenile literature. 2. Canada--Social life and customs--
Juvenile literature. I. Title.

GT4813.A2P47 2012
394.262--dc23

2012004066

Crabtree Publishing Company

www.crabtreebooks.com   1-800-387-7650

Printed in Canada/042012/KR20120316

Published in Canada
Crabtree Publishing
616 Welland Ave.
St. Catharines, Ontario
L2M 5V6

Published in the United States
Crabtree Publishing
PMB 59051
350 Fifth Avenue, 59th Floor
New York, New York 10118

Published in the United Kingdom
Crabtree Publishing
Maritime House
Basin Road North, Hove
BN41 1WR

Published in Australia
Crabtree Publishing
3 Charles Street
Coburg North
VIC 3058

Contents

What is Victoria Day?

Victoria Day is a public holiday that is celebrated in Canada. It is held on the first Monday before May 25. Many Canadians get the day off from work or school.

This juggler is performing at a Victoria Day celebration in Toronto, Ontario.

DID YOU KNOW?

Victoria Day is sometimes called the Sovereign's Birthday. A sovereign is a person who rules over a country, such as a king or queen.

Over 100 years ago, Victoria Day began as a celebration of Queen Victoria's birthday. Queen Victoria was the ruler of Great Britain and Canada at that time. Today, Canada celebrates other British **monarch**'s birthdays on this day, too. Many Canadians enjoy the warm weather on Victoria Day and celebrate outdoors at parks or in their own backyards.

● Many Canadians spend Victoria Day planting flowers or gardens outdoors.

Commonwealth of Nations

Over 200 years ago, Canada was governed, or ruled, by Great Britain. Many people from Great Britain moved to Canada to start the colony. A colony is a territory owned by another country that is faraway, such as Britain. The British Empire was a large group of colonies owned by Great Britain. Today, Great Britain is called the United Kingdom.

- Great Britain is the ninth largest island in the world.

In 1867, Canada became an **independent** country. Canada still has ties to Britain, but is no longer ruled by it. Today, Canada belongs to the Commonwealth of Nations. This is a group of countries that once belonged to the British Empire. People in Canada still take part in many British traditions because of Canada's British **heritage**.

Canadian military troops celebrate the Queen's birthday in Ottawa, Ontario, in 1868 by firing guns into the air.

DID YOU KNOW?

The Commonwealth of Nations is made up of two billion people from 54 different countries.

Queen Victoria

Queen Victoria was born on May 24, 1819. She ruled the British Empire, including Canada, from 1837 until 1901. Queen Victoria's birthday was celebrated in Canada since the beginning of her **reign**. In 1845, her birthday, May 24, was declared a holiday.

- Queen Victoria began ruling the British Empire when she was 18 years old.

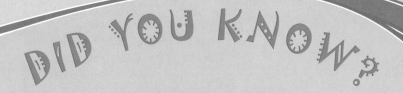

DID YOU KNOW?

Queen Victoria ruled the British Empire for almost 64 years. She holds the record for longest reign of any British monarch, and longest reign for any woman monarch in history!

Queen Victoria's birthday was celebrated on May 24, unless it fell on a Sunday. The queen did not want her birthday celebrations to stop Canadians from going to church on Sunday. People would then celebrate the queen's birthday on May 25 instead.

In 1887, Queen Victoria celebrated 50 years of reign with a Golden Jubilee celebration.

Queen Elizabeth II

Queen Elizabeth II is the current queen of Canada. She was born on April 21, 1926. She has been Canada's monarch since 1952. In 1952, Queen Elizabeth's birthday was celebrated in Canada in June. It is still celebrated in June in the United Kingdom. In 1953, Canada switched her birthday celebration to Victoria Day instead.

● Queen Elizabeth II celebrates her Diamond Jubilee in 2012. Diamond Jubilee means she has reigned for 60 years!

DID YOU KNOW?

Queen Victoria was Queen Elizabeth's great-great-grandmother.

Queen Elizabeth is also queen of the United Kingdom and 15 other Commonwealth countries. Up until now, the reign has been passed from the monarch to the first-born son. According to a new law, the first child born to the monarch, whether it is a son or a daughter, will now be able to **inherit** the throne.

● When Elizabeth is no longer queen, her oldest son Charles, The Prince of Wales, will become king.

Canada's Tradition

Canadians honor traditions and celebrations such as Victoria Day, even though a British monarch no longer rules Canada. A tradition is a custom that has been handed down from past generations.

March 2012

Sunday	Monday	Tuesday	Wednesday	Thursday	Friday	Saturday
				1	2	3
4	5	6	7	8	9	10
11	12 Commonwealth Day	13	14	15	16	17
18	19	20	21	22	23	24
25	26	27	28	29	30	31

- Empire Day was later renamed Commonwealth Day and is celebrated on the second Monday in March.

DID YOU KNOW?

Empire Day was a holiday that was introduced in 1899. It was celebrated by schoolchildren on the last school day before May 24. It was a chance for children to celebrate being part of the British Empire.

Victoria Day is a time for Canadians to remember their British heritage. It is also a time to honor other members of the royal family such as Queen Elizabeth. Canadians take great pride in their ties to the royal family. Even the queen's grandson, William, and his new wife, Kate, are a big attraction in Canada.

Prince William and Kate Middleton were married on April 29, 2011. Their first trip to Canada as newlyweds attracted hundreds of thousands of admirers.

13

God Save the Queen

God save our gracious Queen,
Long live our noble Queen,
God Save the Queen:
Send her victorious,
Happy and glorious,
Long to reign over us,
God Save the Queen.

O Lord, our God, arise,
Scatter thine enemies,
And make them fall:
Confound their politics,
Frustrate their knavish tricks,
On thee our hopes we fix:
God save us all.

Thy choicest gifts in store,
On her be pleased to pour;
Long may she reign:
May she defend our laws,
An ever give us cause
To sing with heart and voice
God save the Queen.

"God Save the Queen" is Canada's royal **anthem**. It is a **patriotic** song that Canadians sing on special days, such as Victoria Day and when members of the royal family visit. The song is actually called "God Save the King," but king is changed to queen when a female monarch reigns.

DID YOU KNOW?

Canada has written its own special verse of "God Save the Queen," that was not included in the original words of the song.

14

The song, "God Save the Queen," is over 250 years old. The United Kingdom and other Commonwealth countries, such as Australia, also use the song as their royal anthem.

Canada creates special collector's stamps and coins that celebrate Queen Elizabeth's golden and diamond jubilees.

CANADA

Golden Jubilee
50 ans de règne

National Holiday

• David Johnston is Canada's governor general. The governor general represents the royal monarch in Canada when he or she is not in the country.

Queen Victoria's birthday has been celebrated in Canada ever since she took the throne in 1837. In 1845, her birthdate was declared a holiday in Canada. In 1901, after Queen Victoria passed away, the Canadian government passed a law making the queen's birthday a **national** holiday under the name Victoria Day.

DID YOU KNOW?

Canada is the only Commonwealth country to celebrate Victoria Day on May 24. Other Commonwealth countries, such as Australia, celebrate the monarch's birthday on the second Monday in June.

Queen Elizabeth II's profile graces Canadian coins, such as this "loonie" or one dollar coin.

In 1952, a law was passed by the government of Canada making Victoria Day the first Monday before May 25. Victoria Day is now always on this day. In many provinces, it is a **statutory** holiday. This means that schools, banks, and government offices are closed for the holiday.

Victoria Day Weekend

Many Canadian families enjoy the first barbecue of the year on the Victoria Day weekend.

Canadians look forward to the Victoria Day holiday because for many it means a three-day weekend. Most people get Saturdays and Sundays off from work or school. Victoria Day is always held on a Monday. This gives most Canadians a long weekend by getting three days off in a row.

DID YOU KNOW?

Some Canadians call the Victoria Day long weekend the May Two-Four. "Two-four" stands for the 24th—the day of Queen Victoria's birthday!

The Victoria Day long weekend is the perfect time for Canadians to get ready for the summer. Many people plant flowers or start planting their vegetable gardens. Others enjoy the warmer weather by camping, hiking, or just spending time outdoors.

Camping is a favorite Canadian pastime, especially on the Victoria Day weekend.

The Royal Union Flag

Some Canadians fly Britain's national flag called the Royal Union Flag, or Union Jack, on Victoria Day to celebrate Canada's British heritage. The Royal Union Flag was first flown in Canada over 400 years ago. It was Canada's national flag until 1965.

Each Canadian province has its own flag. Manitoba's flag has a Royal Union flag pattern in the top, left-hand corner.

DID YOU KNOW?

The Royal Union flag design is on the provincial flags for British Columbia, Manitoba, and Ontario.

The Royal Union Jack is proudly flown in Canada on Victoria Day.

The Royal Union Jack is flown on Victoria Day at all government buildings that are able to fly two flags. Canada's national flag, the red maple leaf, must fly, but if there is another pole the Royal Union Jack flag will join it.

Fireworks

Canadians get a bang out of Victoria Day when they celebrate by watching fireworks displays, or shows. Fireworks displays take place in different cities throughout Canada. One of the largest in Canada is held in Ottawa, Ontario.

Ashbridges Bay Park is a popular spot to view fireworks on Victoria Day in Toronto, Ontario.

DID YOU KNOW?

Different cities across Canada such as Toronto, Ontario, hold fireworks displays for Victoria Day.

The biggest fireworks display takes place in Ottawa, Ontario.

Ottawa is the capital of Canada. The city holds a Victoria Day festival that begins 10 days before Victoria Day. The festival includes live music, a midway with rides and games, and a tulip display. On Victoria Day at 10:15 p.m., the fireworks begin and close out the festival for another year.

23

Victoria, British Columbia

Victoria is the capital city of the Canadian province of British Columbia. It was named after Queen Victoria on June 10, 1843. It was originally named Fort Victoria and began as a small trading post for the Hudson's Bay Company. In 1852, its name was changed to just Victoria.

The British Columbia **Parliament** buildings were built in Victoria, British Columbia, in 1896.

Victoria Day celebrations in Victoria include Canada's largest Victoria Day parade. It is a 3-hour long parade. Marching bands, floats, clowns, and other entertainers **participate** in the parade. The parade can be watched on television, too. Over 100,000 people look forward to watching the parade on Victoria Day.

- An entertainer rides an old-fashioned bicycle during the 2011 Victoria Day parade in Victoria, B.C.

DID YOU KNOW?

Victoria, British Columbia, is one of the oldest cities in Western Canada.

Bread & Cheese Day

First Nations Canadians from the Six Nations Reserve celebrate the May 24 holiday as Bread and Cheese Day. The Six Nations Reserve is near Brantford, Ontario. On this day, people gather at the reserve for free bread and cheese. Many gather to watch a Victoria Day parade, and enjoy a midway with games and rides.

- First Nations people celebrate Victoria Day with gifts of bread and cheese.

DID YOU KNOW?

Over 2,000 pounds (907 kg) of cheese is served on Bread and Cheese Day at the Six Nations' Gaylord Powless Arena.

Queen Victoria started the tradition of giving to the First Nations community in 1837. She gave First Nations people blankets and other gifts to thank them for fighting with Britain in the **War of 1812**. The tradition stopped when she died in 1901. In 1924, members of the Six Nations started the tradition of gift-giving once again.

A photo taken in 1882 shows the last three Six Nations warriors who fought with the British in the War of 1812.

National Patriots' Day

Canadians in Quebec celebrate the Victoria Day holiday as National Patriots Day. In Quebec, it is not a day to honor the monarch of Canada. Instead, Canadians from Quebec honor French-Canadian patriots who fought against the British in 1837 and 1838. Patriots are people who love and fight for their country.

French Canadians celebrate National Patriots' Day on the first Monday before May 25.

In the 1800s, many Canadians were from Britain or France. The French Canadians didn't agree with how the country was being run. They rebelled, or fought, against the British in the Rebellion of 1837, but the French lost.

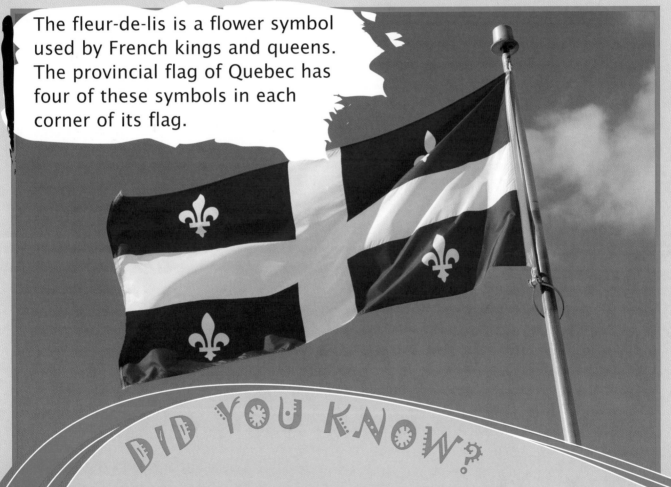

The fleur-de-lis is a flower symbol used by French kings and queens. The provincial flag of Quebec has four of these symbols in each corner of its flag.

DID YOU KNOW?

National Patriots' Day in Quebec began in 2003. Before that, Quebec celebrated Victoria Day as Dollard's Day. Dollard des Ormeaux was a French soldier who lived in Canada over 400 years ago.

Victoria Day Quiz

1. What does Victoria Day celebrate?

2. When is Queen Elizabeth's birthday celebrated in Canada?

3. How do First Nations people celebrate Victoria Day?

4. Victoria is the capital city of British Columbia. Who is it named after?

5. What is Canada's royal anthem?

Answers: 1. The birthday of the queen or king of Canada. 2. Victoria Day, or the first Monday before May 25. 3. With bread and cheese. 4. Queen Victoria. 5. God Save the King (or Queen).

Glossary

anthem A happy song that shows love for a country

First Nations One of the first peoples to live in Canada

heritage The beliefs, customs, and traditions passed on from generation to generation

independent Not controlled by another

inherit To receive something from an ancestor

monarch A person who is born into power and rules over others

national The combined states, provinces, or territories that belong to one country

Parliament A group of people that make the laws for a province or country

participate To take part in

patriotic Showing respect and love for a person's country

reign The power or rule of a monarch

statutory Having to do something because it is a law

War of 1812 A war between the United States and the British Empire

Index